The Beeman

Laurie Krebs · illustrated by Melissa Iwai

NATIONAL GEOGRAPHIC
WASHINGTON, D.C.

Text copyright © 2002 Laurie Krebs
Illustrations copyright © 2002 Melissa Iwai

Published by the National Geographic Society.
All rights reserved. Reproduction of the whole or any
part of the contents without written permission from
the National Geographic Society is strictly prohibited.

Illustrations are in acrylic on board.
Book design by Bea Jackson
Display and body text of the book are set in Comic Sans.

Library of Congress Cataloging-in-Publication Data
Krebs, Laurie.
    The Beeman / by Laurie Krebs ; illustrated by Melissa Iwai.
        p. cm.
Summary: In rhyming text, a child describes the work
Grandpa does to take care of honeybees and harvest the
honey they make.
        ISBN 0-7922-7224-2 (Hardcover)
[1. Beekeepers—Fiction. 2. Bee culture—Fiction. 3. Honeybees
—Fiction. 4. Grandfathers—Fiction. 5. Stories in rhyme.]
I. Iwai, Melissa, ill. II. Title
        PZ8.3.K867 Be 2002
        [E]—dc21   2001003540

One of the world's largest nonprofit
scientific and educational organizations,
the National Geographic Society was
founded in 1888 "for the increase and
diffusion of geographic knowledge."
Fulfilling this mission, the Society educates and inspires
millions every day through its magazines, books, television
programs, videos, maps and atlases, research grants, the
National Geographic Bee, teacher workshops, and innovative
classroom materials. The Society is supported through
membership dues, charitable gifts, and income from the
sale of its educational products. This support is vital to
National Geographic's mission to increase global under-
standing and promote conservation of our planet through
exploration, research, and education.

NATIONAL GEOGRAPHIC SOCIETY
1145 17th Street N.W.
Washington, D.C. 20036-4688
U.S.A.
Visit the Society's Web site: www.nationalgeographic.com

Printed in the United States of America

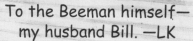

To the Beeman himself—
my husband Bill. —LK

To Chris, through whom
I met the Krebs, through
whom I met the bees. —MI

Here is my Grandpa,
who's known in our town as
the Beeman.

Here is his jacket,
with zippered-up hood
that covers his face
just the way that it should
when he visits his hives as
the Beeman.

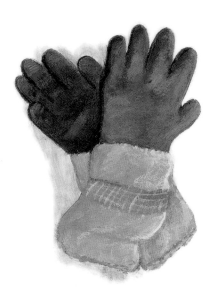

Here are his gloves
made of cotton and leather,
protecting his hands
in all kinds of weather
when he tends to his hives as
the Beeman.

Here is the beehive,
where all the bees sleep,
tucked into a box
called a shallow or deep
and then placed on a bench by
the Beeman.

Here is the smoker
that quiets the bees

and a hive tool that opens
the beehive with ease

for a much closer look by
the Beeman.

Here is the queen bee,
who does her job well
and lays tiny eggs
in a six-sided cell.
"She's the heart of the hive,"
says the Beeman.

Here is a drone bee
with big bulging eyes
and a large appetite
supporting his size.
"He mates with the queen," adds
the Beeman.

Here are the workers,
ten thousand or more,
who gather the nectar
to bring back and store
in honeycomb cells for
the Beeman.

Here are the house bees
with swift-moving wings
that dry up the nectar
a worker bee brings,
making honey for me and
the Beeman.

Here's the extractor,
its "clickety-clack"
removing the honey
from frames on its rack
and filling up jars for
the Beeman.

Here's some of the honey
returned to the hive.
It's food for the bees
to help them survive
the long winter days near
the Beeman.

Here are the bees
protected from harm,
inside the hive,
huddled cozy and warm,
"So they'll be here next year,"
says the Beeman.

Here is the wagon
filled up to the brim
with bottles of honey
collected by him
and brought to the house by
the Beeman.

Here are the muffins,
all warm and delicious
and dripping with honey
on Grandma's best dishes.

I'm glad that my grandpa's the Beeman.